CHERISH
TODAY

CHERISH TODAY

A CELEBRATION OF LIFE'S MOMENTS

by KRISTINA EVANS

illustrations by
Bryan COLLIER

JUMP AT THE SUN
HYPERION BOOKS FOR CHILDREN
NEW YORK

In memory of Dr. C. Kermit Phelps, thank you
for carving out my path.
And to the extraordinary students of P.S. 161:
Never Stop Dreaming!
—K.E.

To our daughter, Haley, an amazing
reminder to cherish each moment
—B.C.

Stand up, be proud, hip hip hooray!
You've accomplished your goals and you're on your way.
I know you feel awestruck, ecstatic, and thrilled.
You've completed this round; I admire your will.

The gifts that you have shine now more than ever.
You are loaded with wit, and you've proven you're clever.
You've been given the tools to build on your dreams.
You have just scored a point for the game-winning team.

The game is now over, but there's more to do,
And your teammates are no longer right beside you.
Which way are you going? Now who's got your back?
If you keep pushing forward, you'll find a new track.

Let's be honest; there may be some days
When your life will resemble an underground maze.
Every time you go out, you'll be routed back in.
Every light in the tunnel reveals a dead end.

This is when feelings start to get hyped.

Your heart begins pounding; should you forfeit this fight?

You can still join the race, but you can't always lead.

And it may take some time to find your own speed.

Some days it might feel like your path isn't clear.

Our prayers are behind you and we'll help you steer.

Will you stay focused and follow your heart?

Even though it may lead you straight off the chart?

Just remember to honor those who came before.

They carved out the path, now you open the door.

You can do it! You hold the key

To persevere and uphold our rich legacy.

Exciting adventures lie ahead in your path.

For every tear shed, you are promised two laughs.

So just take it slow, one day at a time,

And you'll find that your path is truly divine.

It won't be easy; you'll be put to the test.

But challenge is worth it when you find yourself blessed.

There's no right or wrong way, you must pull from within.

You've finished the warm-up . . . let the true race begin.

On your mark; get set; ready; and *run!*

You've inspired so many with a job well done.

But before you set off, just let me say:

The future's tomorrow,
Cherish today!